D1112317

Peanut Butter

A Traditional Song
Illustrated by Robin Oz

▣ GoodYearBooks

PORTSMOUTH PUBLIC LIBRARY
601 COURT STREET
PORTSMOUTH, VA 23704

Econo-Clad 4-12-01 4.5

Copy 1

R TR
02

Peanut, peanut butter.

Jelly!

Peanut, peanut butter.

Jelly!

First, you take the grapes
and you squish them.

Squish them!

Then, you take the peanuts
and you mash them.

Mash them!

Next, you take the bread
and you spread it.

Spread it!

Last, you take the sandwich
and you eat it.

Eat it!

PORTSMOUTH PUBLIC LIBRARY
601 COURT STREET
PORTSMOUTH, VA 23704

Peanut, peanut butter. Jelly!

Peanut, peanut butter. Jelly!

8

RTR Copy 1

Oz.
Peanut Butter.

PORTSMOUTH PUBLIC LIBRARY

3 3230 00521 0707

373105

PORTSMOUTH PUBLIC LIBRARY
601 COURT STREET
PORTSMOUTH, VA 23704